Satchmo's BLUES

BY ALAN SCHROEDER

ILLUSTRATED BY FLOYD COOPER

A Picture Yearling Book

Louis Armstrong once wrote that, when he was a boy, he "saw a little cornet in a pawn shop window—five dollars. My luck was just right. . . . I saved fifty cents a week and bought the horn. All dirty—but was soon pretty to me. . . . From then I was a mess and tootin' away. I kept that horn for a long time."

This book is based upon that little-known incident.

Published by
Bantam Doubleday Dell Books for Young Readers
a division of
Random House, Inc.
1540 Broadway
New York, New York 10036

ISBN: 0-440-41472-5
Reprinted by arrangement with Doubleday Books for Young Readers
Printed in the United States of America
February 1999
10 9 8 7 6 5 4 3 2 1

To Rick Gydesen
A.S.

For my uncle, Billy Williams
F.C.

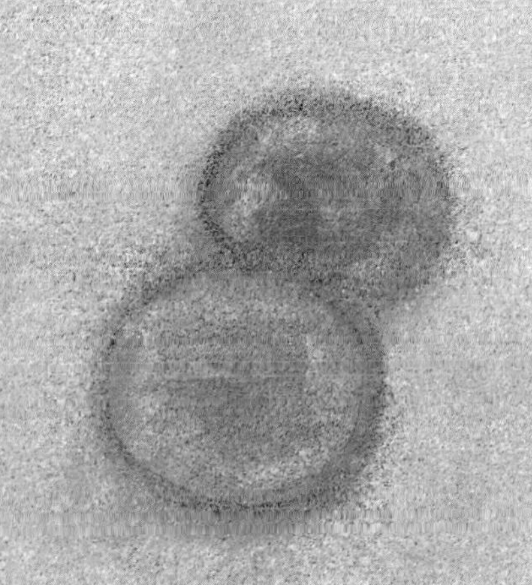

It was a hot night in New Orleans, and Economy Hall was jumping. Louis stood outside and listened to the band. The pianist was playing "Panama Rag," and whenever he could, Louis would get down on his knees and peek under the big swinging doors. Economy Hall was a great place. The tables were clean, the peanuts were fresh, and the Eagle Band played some of the best jazz in New Orleans.

In the corner, Mama Haines had put out her pipe and was getting ready to sing "Ham Tree Barbecue." Louis could hardly wait. Just then, the bartender looked up. He stopped wiping the beer mugs and grinned.

"Git out of here, Louis," he called. He pronounced it the French way—Lou-ee—the way people in New Orleans always did. "You go on home. You don't be hangin' round no gin mill."

But Louis didn't want to leave. The music was too good, and besides, Bunk Johnson was in the band. Every Friday night, Bunk would show up in his spiffy red shirt and blow his cornet till the roof trembled.

Every now and then, Bunk would catch sight of Louis' head underneath the swinging doors and right away he'd let out a big, terrific grin like he'd died and gone to Heaven. Moments like those, Louis could feel his toes tingle.

Finally, around ten o'clock, Louis' mama had to come and take him home.

"I don't know what I'm going to do with you, child," she scolded. "I worried myself sick wonderin' where you were."

As they mounted the porch steps, Louis was hoping there'd be some red beans and rice in Mama's kettle, but when he lifted the lid and peered in, it was empty. So was the kitchen cupboard.

"Isn't there anything to eat?" he asked.

Mama shook her head. "I'm sorry, baby." She reached into her pocket and took out two oranges. "One for you and one for your sister." She saw the sad look on Louis' face. "Don't worry," she told him. "We'll have more tomorrow. I promise."

Louis said nothing. He took the orange and went to bed.

Louis and his family lived on Perdido Street, "back o' town." It was a tough neighborhood, full of broken bottles and mangy dogs and kicked-in fences. But Louis didn't mind. At night when the lanterns were lit and Willie Reed brought out his fiddle, it was just like being at Economy Hall, with everyone clapping and dancing on boards:

"Mr. Jefferson Lord—

Play that barbershop chord!"

"Back o' town," everyone had a musical instrument of some kind—a clarinet, or a banjo, or maybe just an old pot someone had turned into a drum. But Louis didn't want a clarinet or a banjo. He wanted to blow a horn, just like Bunk Johnson. A real cornet, brass, with valves so quiet they whispered. But that took money, and Mama didn't have any. Not enough for a cornet anyway.

"You're gonna have to wait," she told Louis. "Now come on, help me hang up this washin'."

Every Saturday, Louis and his sister, Beatrice, had to help Mama with the laundry. It was Louis' job to keep the iron hot. The small kitchen smelled of lye and starch, and the hands on the clock moved as slow as molasses. Outside, Louis could hear laughter and shouting, and a pack of happy dogs barking.

"Aren't we done yet?" he kept asking.

"In a bit," Mama would answer. "Come on now, let's sing a song. That'll make the time go quick."

And, tapping the stove with an old wooden spoon, she started singing "Little Black Baby." Beatrice giggled and Louis, crouching down, pretended he was blowing his horn right on the hot coals. Outside, the dogs went crazy with their barking.

"Let's do another one!" Beatrice cried, and sure enough, they did. They kept it up all afternoon, washing and ironing to the beat of the music.

Finally, just as the sun was setting, Mama folded the last shirt, ran a handkerchief across her brow, and smiled.

"We're done," she said, nodding.

That was all Louis needed to hear. Instantly, he took off lickety-split for the door.

"Come back here!" Mama called, but Louis was already gone, tearing down the dusty alley, hightailing it over the fence, and skidding to a stop in front of Sister Leola's. By that time, the food table was already full and the men were laying down wooden planks for dancing.

Saturday night was Rag Night, and Sister Leola's was the only place to be. Before the dancing began, Leola made sure everyone had brought something for the food table.

"Why, you lazy thing!" she would scold when someone showed up empty-handed. "Git on home and bring back somethin', or honey, I'm gonna whomp your head! This here's Rag Night, not a Red Cross handout!"

Louis couldn't take his eyes off the food table. Marandy's biscuits were piping hot and the heavy pitchers of lemonade were ice-cold.

The band always started off with a great number, like "Dixie Flyer," and, grabbing a handful of cornbread, Louis stood and watched the dancing.

One night, a paper lantern caught fire, sending a shower of sparks over the crowd. Everyone cheered, and instantly, the cornet man started playing "Hot Time in the Old Town Tonight." Giselle, the voodoo lady, let out a huge belly laugh.

"Well, don't just stand there," she cried, pushing Louis forward. "Scorch those boards!"

Louis tried to move his feet in time to the music, but he was a lousy scorcher. And besides, he didn't want to dance—he wanted to play the cornet. He wanted to be like Bunk Johnson: aim his horn straight up at the night sky and set the stars spinning.

"That takes lungs," Leola told him. "Why don't you dance, instead? Here, give me your shoes."

Louis did, and, laughing, Leola glued a penny onto the heel of each one.

"Now you got taps," she said, and sure enough, every time Louis took a step, a tap jumped out. *Tap! Tap! Tap!*

It was fun, for a while. But it wasn't as much fun as a cornet.

One day, right off Bourbon Street Louis saw a horn sitting in a pawnshop window. It was a humdinger, all bright and sassy, just begging to be bought. The cardboard sign said $5. Louis turned away. He could never come up with that much money.

"It's not fair!" he thought. Everyone else had a musical instrument. Even Santiago, the pie man, had a little horn hanging from his wooden cart. People came flocking when they heard his familiar *toot-toot-ta-toot-toot*.

The next time Santiago came "back o' town," Louis ran up and tugged on his sleeve.

"Can I blow that horn, mister?" he asked eagerly.

The pie man handed it to him with a grin. Louis whipped the horn up to his lips and blew.

Nothing happened. Just a flat, spitting sound. *Pppbhbh....*

Everybody laughed, especially Santiago. Louis tried again. This time, the noise was even worse.

Santiago reached down and took the horn away.

"I thought you said you could blow it, Louis."

Louis frowned. "I thought I could."

That made everyone laugh even harder.

But Louis didn't give up. He wanted to turn that awful *pppbhbh* into something wonderful—something so hot and jazzy that everyone would come running.

"And I'm gonna do it, too," he said to himself.

Two weeks later, the horn was still in the pawnshop window. Louis wanted to go inside, but the man behind the counter didn't look any too friendly. The cardboard sign still said $5.

"That horn is mine," Louis whispered, pressing his nose against the window. "It's gotta be mine!"

Every afternoon, when he got home from school, Louis stood in front of the mirror and practiced his blowing. He pretended he was Bunk Johnson, raising the roof with his high C's.

"What's you doin' with your lips?" Mama asked. "You look like a fish."

"I'm blowin' my horn," Louis told her.

Mama shook her head. "I don't see any horn."

But Louis could—and it was a beauty.

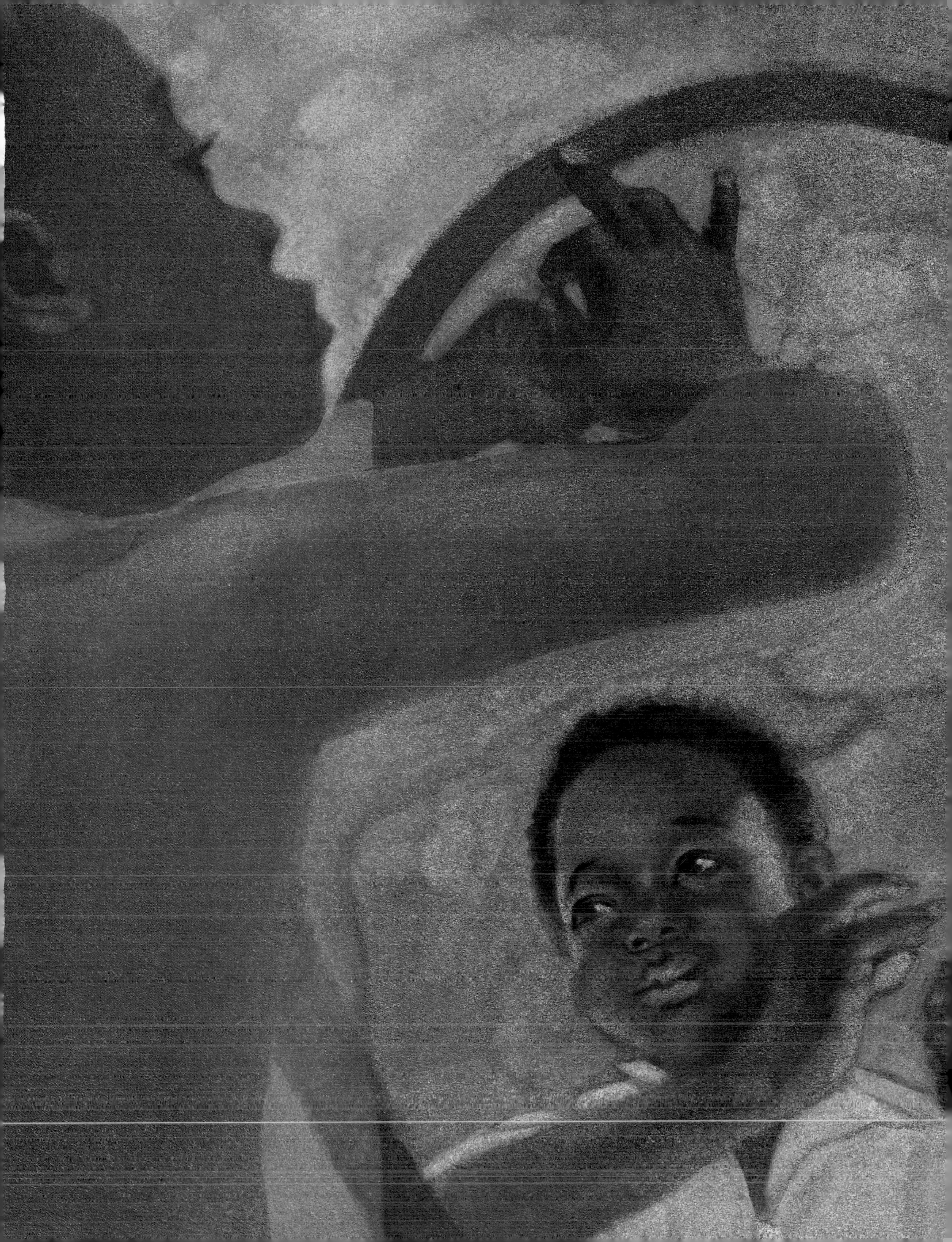

Anytime there was a parade in New Orleans, Louis joined right in.

"Go on, get out of here, boy," the marchers told him, but that didn't stop Louis. He'd kick out his legs and fall in right behind the Excelsior Brass Band. One time, Bunk Johnson saw him from the sidewalk and waved. Louis' grin must have stretched from ear to ear. He didn't have a uniform—he didn't even have a horn—but Louis just had to be the proudest stepper in the whole parade.

That spring, he did everything he could to earn five dollars. He sold rags and coal, and ran errands for the neighbors. Twice a week, he went "front o' town" to the produce markets and poked through the trash barrels.

"You're not going to find a horn that way," his sister Beatrice said, laughing.

"Go away," Louis said. He wasn't looking for a horn—he was hunting for spoiled onions. Using a little knife, he'd cut

out the rotten parts, dump the good parts in a sack, and sell them to the restaurants on Perdido Street. Five cents a bag.

"Where'd you get these onions, boy?" a man asked suspiciously.

"I grow 'em," Louis said. "I eat 'em, too. Want to smell my breath?"

The man stared at him for a moment, then laughed. "Why, you're sassier'n blazes! I like that! I'll take two bags."

Every Sunday, Mama took Louis and Beatrice to Elder Cozy's church. Louis could hardly sit still, listening to the rich gospel music around him. Mama closed her eyes and rocked back and forth, clapping her hands. During the sermon, Louis pretended he was messing with his horn.

"Quit makin' that fish face!" Mama whispered.

But Louis couldn't quit. Blowing that horn was all he could think about. Any week now, he'd walk into that pawnshop and plunk down his money. He had four dollars now—only one dollar to go.

Still, that was a lot of onions to sell.

On Decoration Day, Louis took the trolley to the Girod Cemetery. There, he pulled weeds and polished the tombstones for tips. He earned fifty-five cents that day. Heading home, Louis felt tired but happy. He'd have his horn by the end of the week!

He was surprised to see Mama waiting for him out on the front stoop. She looked worried.

"Today is your sister's birthday," she said quietly. "You know every year I make a mess of jambalaya, but that costs money, and right now I'm low. I need a quarter, Louis."

She held out her hand. For a second, Louis felt like bursting into tears. Why was she asking for a whole quarter? Didn't she know he was trying to save his money? Didn't she care?

"But Mama—"

"It's not for me, it's for your sister."

Louis pointed to his mother's apron pocket, where she kept her money. "You have enough," he said.

"I may and I may not. I think you need to chip in, Louis. You can't always be thinkin' about yourself and what you want." She touched his shoulder gently. "And, Louis . . . you know how much you love my jambalaya."

It was a hard choice. Louis stuck his hand in his pants pocket and fished around for a quarter. Why, why was Mama asking him to do this?

"Here," he said, quickly handing her the money. And before Mama could say thank you, Louis ran into the house, tears streaming down his cheeks.

That evening, Mama fixed a huge pot of her best jambalaya: shrimp and crab, and thick slices of spicy Cajun sausage.

"This'll keep your jaws a-jumpin'." She laughed, spooning the jambalaya into three big soup bowls.

Louis ate till his stomach was fixing to burst. He was glad now he'd given Mama the quarter. There was nothing "back o' town" to beat the taste of good jambalaya.

An hour later, after the dishes had been washed, Mama came out onto the stoop. Louis was sitting there quietly, looking up at the sky.

"I 'preciate what you did," Mama told him. "I know you were savin' that quarter for somethin' else." She paused, like she wasn't sure what to say next. "Here, I have something to give you. Hold out your hand."

Louis did. Mama dropped a silver dollar into his palm.

"I'm tired of seein' that fish face," she said to him, grinning. "It's time you got a real horn."

At last, Louis had his five dollars! He didn't even wait to put on his shoes. He ran as fast as he could down to the pawnshop and flung his money on the counter. The nickels spun like crazy on the wood.

"What do you want?" the owner asked. "I'm closin'."

"I want that horn in the window," Louis said.

The man grunted. "That horn is five dollars, sonny."

"That horn is mine!" Louis said proudly.

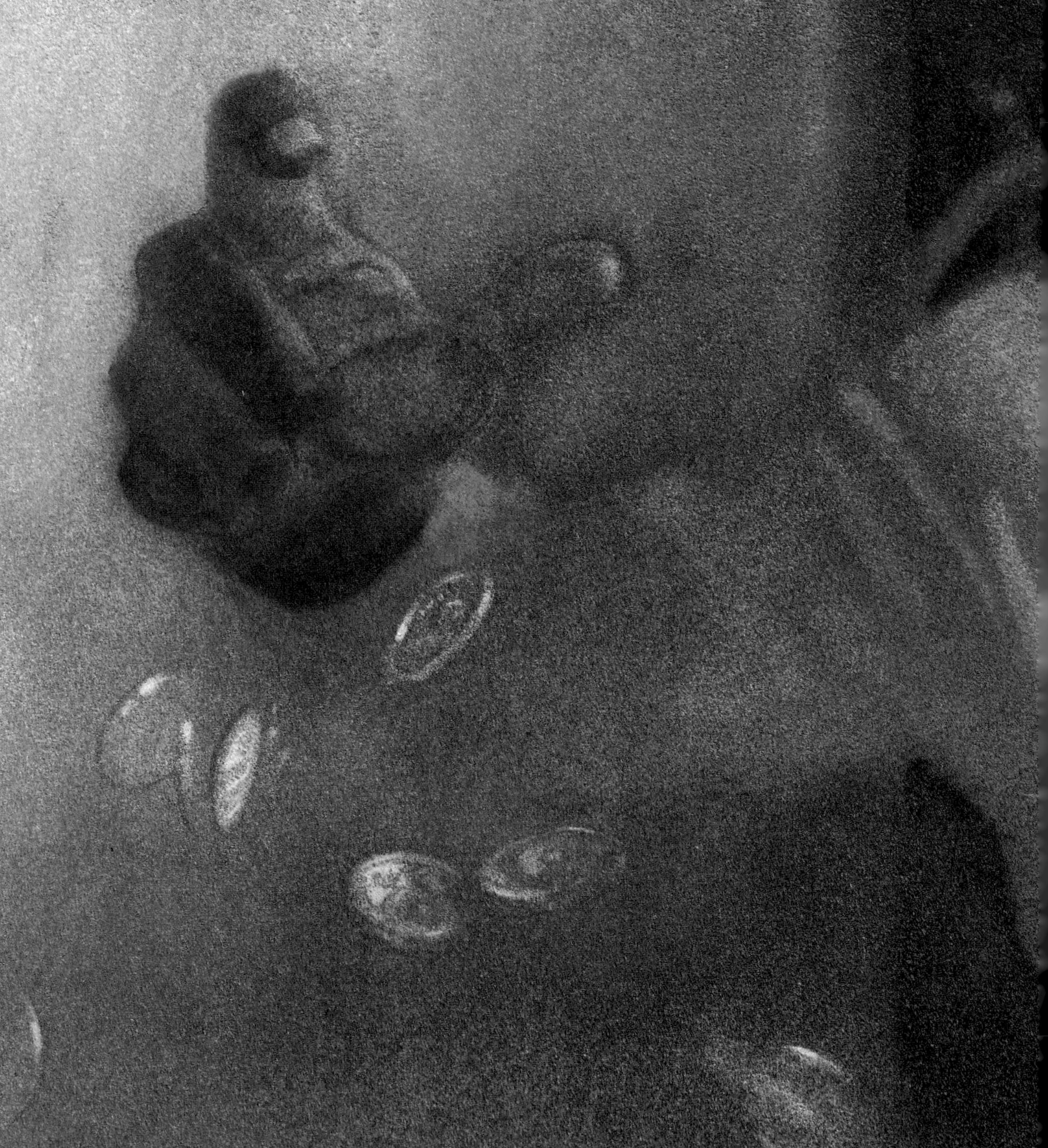

Leaving the pawnshop, Louis felt ten feet tall. Underneath a streetlamp, he got a good look at his horn. Sure, it was full of dings and dents, but he didn't care. A little elbow grease and it'd be as good as new.

The air that night was rich with honeysuckle and jazz. Louis leaned up against an old packing crate, pressed his lips to the mouthpiece, and blew.

A moment later, a wonderful sound filled the alley: music. One note, then two, three, four, then a whole cluster, all tripping out over each other. Louis' cheeks puffed out like air bags. He loved the sound he was hearing. It wasn't "Dixie Flyer," but it wasn't *ppphhhh,* either.

"Lou-is!" Mama was calling him in the distance. But he wasn't ready to go home yet. Not by a long shot. He'd waited a long time for this moment.

Leaning back, Louis pointed his horn straight up at the moon.

"Hold on, stars," he whispered. "Someday, I'm gonna blow you right out of the sky."

He propped his elbows on his knees, closed his eyes, and began to play.

AUTHOR'S NOTE

Louis Armstrong went on to become the most famous trumpeter in the history of popular music.

Leaving New Orleans at the age of twenty-one, he traveled north to Chicago, where he began his long and successful recording career. The microphone, and the public, loved Louis. Over the years, his string of hits included "Ain't Misbehavin'," "Tiger Rag," "West End Blues," and "Hello, Dolly!" The film industry was quick to spot Louis' remarkable talent: he appeared in numerous musicals, and by the 1950s he had become an international celebrity, known around the world as Satchmo or Ambassador Satch.

Louis was also a talented composer, writing, among other pieces, "Coal Cart Blues," "Cornet Chop Suey," and "Struttin' with Some Barbecue." His autobiography, *Satchmo: My Life in New Orleans,* appeared in 1954.

Louis Armstrong, the Trumpet King of Swing, died in New York City on July 6, 1971. His gravelly voice and dynamic trumpet playing will never be forgotten.